Families everywhere

All across the world children live in families.

United States of America
Peru
Japan

Who is in your family?

There are many different kinds of family. Here are a few.

Davey lives with his mum and dad, his brother and sisters. His mum took the photo.

Rose and Hannah live with their foster mum and her son.

Ayanfe is adopted. She lives with her dads.

David lives with his mum.

Who is part of your family?

Sam lives with his mums, and his dog Kip.

Mums and dads

Lots of children live with their mum and dad. Some children live with just their mum or dad. Some children live with a step-dad or a step-mum.

Parents and step-parents look after us, especially when we are babies.

They show us how to care for ourselves.

They help us feel better when we are sad.

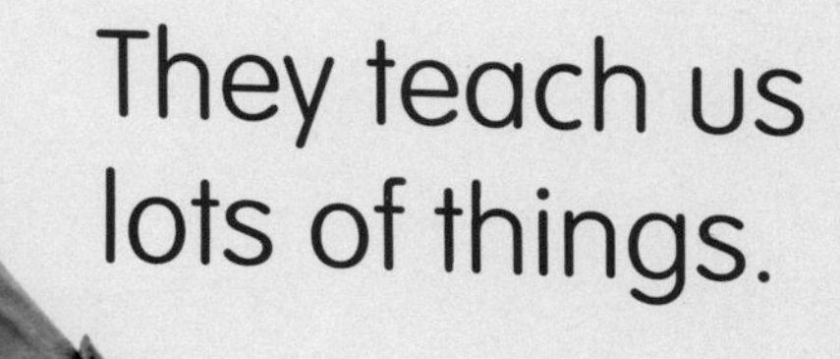

They teach us lots of things.

Going to work

Many mums and dads go out to work to earn money.

Daniel's mum works in a school in the mornings.

Jake's step-dad works on building sites.

What job do you want to do when you grow up?

Arminder's dad travels to his job in an office.

Brothers and sisters

Some of us have brothers and sisters, step-brothers and step-sisters, half-brothers or half-sisters.

I have one sister.

I have one half-brother. He lives with us some of the time.

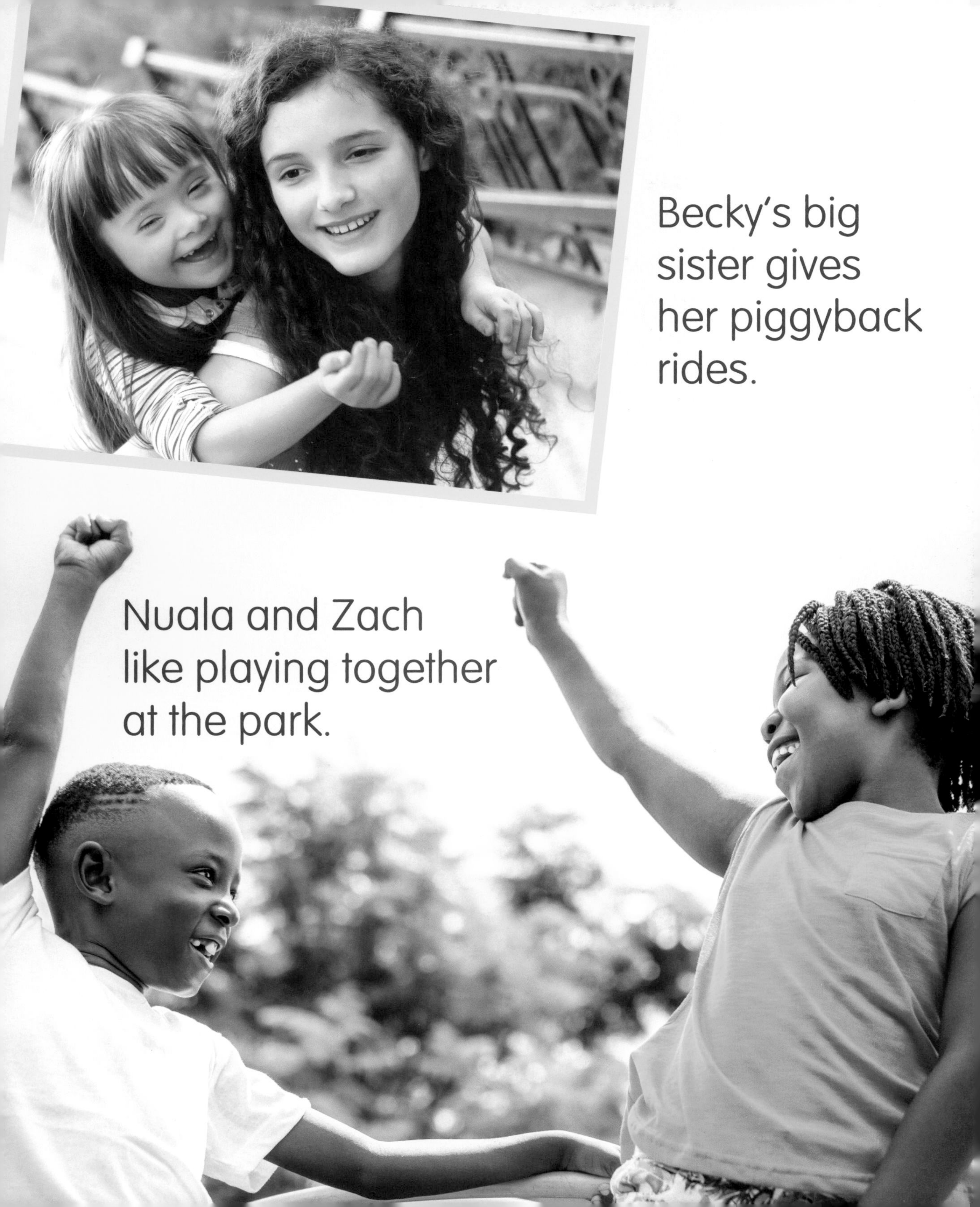

Becky's big sister gives her piggyback rides.

Nuala and Zach like playing together at the park.

Home life

At home families spend time together in all sorts of ways.

Olivia and Lily play with their brother when their mum is busy.

Luke and his dad play video games.

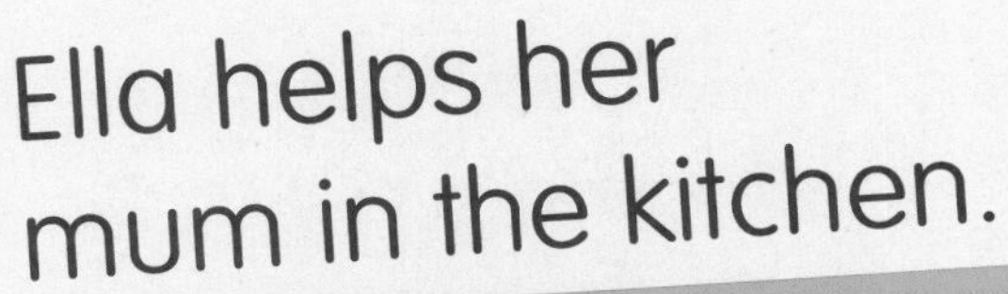

Ella helps her
mum in the kitchen.

What do you
like doing
at home?

Sometimes
Kirstie likes to
find a quiet
place to read
away from
everyone!

Out and about

Some families go out together at weekends. They take holidays and day trips.

I like going for a family walk at the weekend.
Where do you like to go with your family?

Dad and I have fun in the park.
We like days at the seaside.

Celebrations

Families celebrate birthdays, weddings, festivals and other special days together.

Match these words to the correct festival picture: Hanukkah, Christmas, Diwali, Chinese New Year.

4

2

3

1

Which special days do you celebrate with your family?

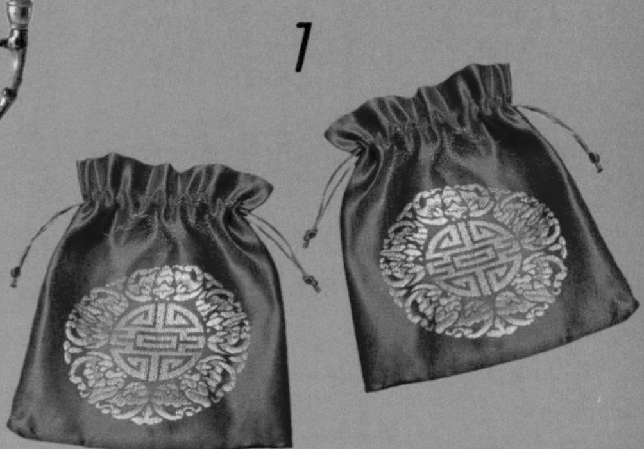

The answers are on page 24.

Grandparents

Grandparents are the parents of your mum and dad.

I call my grandmother Nanny. She is my mum's mum.
What do you call your grandparents?

We talk to our granny on our computer every week.

Preet likes going fishing with her grandad when she visits him.

Other family members

As well as grandparents and even great-grandparents, you may have aunts, uncles and cousins.

Nan
Grandad
Auntie Kim
Uncle David (lives with Aunt Jess)
Dad
Ellie
Me

Here is my family tree. How many cousins have I got?

Your aunts and uncles are the sisters and brothers of your mum and dad. The children of your aunts and uncles are your cousins.

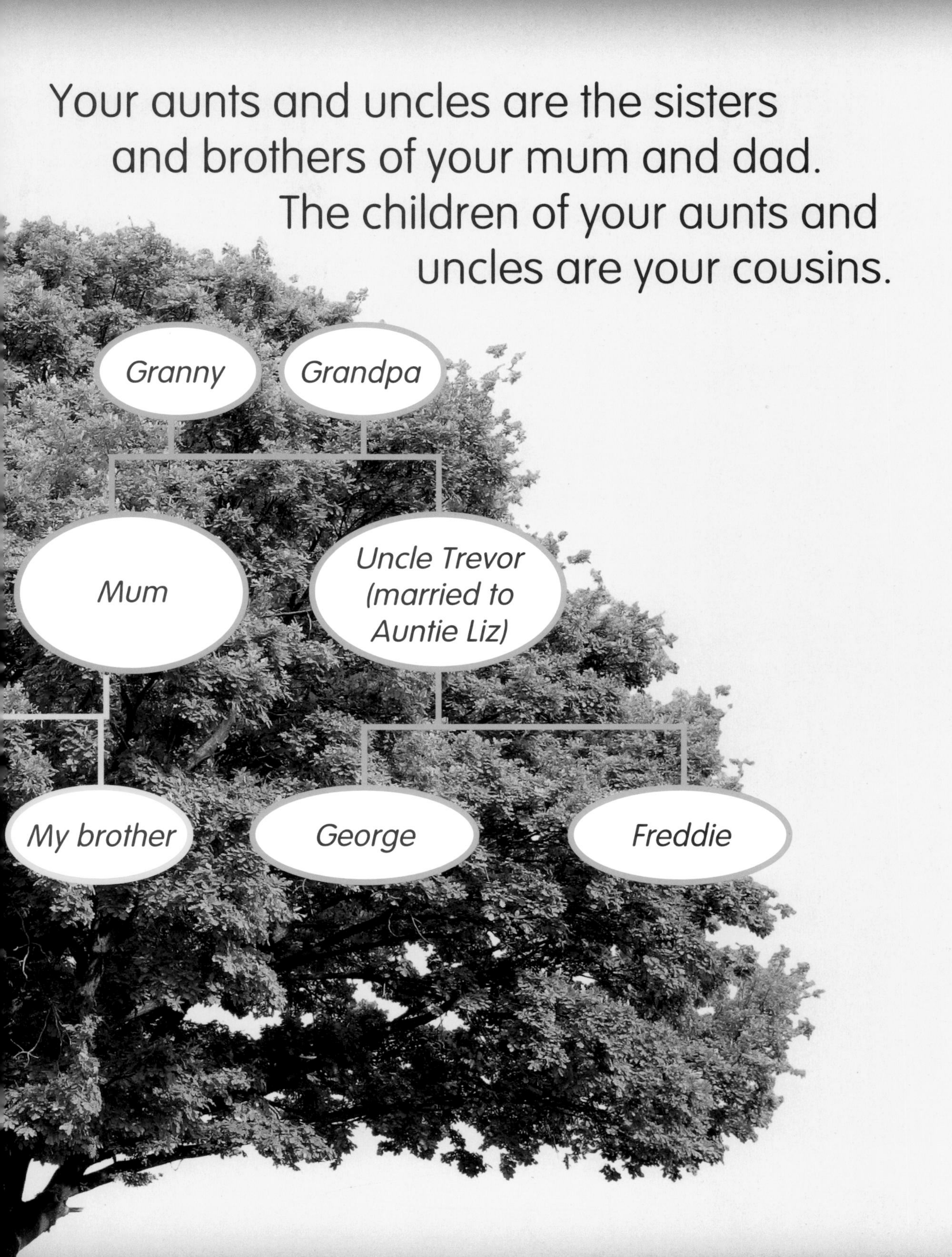
Granny
Grandpa
Mum
Uncle Trevor (married to Auntie Liz)
My brother
George
Freddie

Animal families

People are animals. Some other animals live in family groups.

Elephants live in herds of mothers and their calves.

Lions live in family groups called prides.

Male and female wolves bring up their cubs together in a wolf pack.

Word bank

Adopted

Brothers

Dad

Foster mum

Grandparent

Half-brothe

Lion pride

Mum

Sisters

Index

Answers to the questions on page 17: 1. Chinese New Year; 2. Christmas; 3. Hanukkah; 4. Diwali.